LULU

LULU

ADVENTURES IN A DOG'S LIFE

Sandra Dawes

Staten House

ISBN-13: 979-8-89496-882-7

Cover design by: Harbirz Inc.
Printed in the United States of America

I'm dedicating this book to the dog who was my therapist, personal trainer, yoga buddy, provider of unending entertainment and source material. I love you, Lulu! xoxo

Table of Contents

Acknowledgments

Thank you to Take Me Home Rescue, who introduced Lulu into my life almost twenty years ago. She was a treasure, and I fully enjoyed all 13 and a half years she was in my life. Those experiences inspired this book.

I have heartfelt gratitude to my husband, Satnam. You're my biggest cheerleader and believe in me, even when I doubt myself.

I thank my inner circle for supporting me via WhatsApp messages, calls and IG meme shares. I appreciate you loving me regardless of my wacky traits! xo

Chapter 1: Introduction

Hi! Before you start reading my story, an introduction is necessary. My name is Lulu, and I'm a part black labrador retriever with a mix of border collie. I'm black with a white patch on my chest and frosted paws for my front legs.

My support person says that I have the goofy personality of a labrador and the brains and energy of a border collie. She seems conflicted about whether it's a good thing, but I'm convinced it is.

If you're wondering what a support person (SP for the remainder of my story) is, it's the person rescue dogs like me choose to live with because they need our love and support. I'll tell you all about how I found my SP and our adventures.

I decided to tell my story because I hear her telling people about my adventures, and I want to set the record straight. If you listen to her telling any of these stories, you can fact-check her.

The story starts when I met my support person. I don't remember much before that because I was just a four-month-old pup, but I'll tell you what I've been told.

I'm getting old now, but I always remember the best parts of my adventures and life with my support person and her boyfriend.

Are you ready? Let's go!

Chapter 2: Disclaimer

My SP suggested that I include a disclaimer about my stories. I don't recommend allowing your pet to ingest anything I include in my stories. As you'll learn as you read about my experiences, I'm not your average dog.

My SP suggested creating a YouTube channel, but the boyfriend turned down the idea, saying his heart couldn't encourage my antics (I don't know what that means, but I'm pretty sure he ruined some good fun!

Chapter 3: The Rescue

Okay, I'll be honest; I don't remember much since I was only 4 months old when it happened. Still, I've been told some people from Mississauga drove to Ohio to get me and some other dogs. They say the place was a "kill shelter." I don't know what that means, but I'm glad they got me out because it doesn't sound like good things happen there.

I've been told that when I first got to Canada, I lived with a foster family while my new SP was being found. I would live with someone who needed a dog to lift their spirits. I was excited to see who my person would be.

I was on my best behaviour in my foster home because it was a lot nicer than the place I was in Ohio. I resisted the urge to beg for food and did things to show that I was not the average dog. I might have been young, but I knew early that I was unique, and I couldn't wait to share that with my forever person.

I heard that my potential person was coming to see me and answer some questions so that they could decide if I could go home with them right away. I liked where I was, but I knew it wasn't my forever home and was looking forward to finding it.

The day my potential person was coming was exciting for me. When I heard the doorbell ring, I went with my caregiver to greet them at the door. It was a woman, and her eyes seemed to light up when she saw me. I had a good feeling about this one.

She sat down and spoke with my caregiver, and I made myself part of the conversation. After all, a decision was being made about where I was living and who the heck I was living with!

I immediately connected with her and tested her to see if she was okay with puppy kisses. I was pleasantly surprised that she was more than okay with it. She seemed happier when I did it and gave me lots of rubs. I even took a chance and went on my back. She looked like she gave good tummy rubs, and she did!

When my potential person commented on my cuteness, my caregiver agreed but warned her that I was pretty smart for such a young pup. I wasn't sure if I should be offended or flattered, but I chose to take it as a compliment.

The decision was made that my potential person would be my SP! I was excited to see what my new home looked like.

She put a purple collar on me with a matching purple leash and took me to her car. I hadn't done many car rides then, so I was excited and couldn't stay still. I ended up riding shotgun with her for most of the ride to my new place.

My new home was a one-bedroom condo, much smaller than the old one. The last place I left had a circular driveway and a big backyard!

My new SP also had a floppy-eared rabbit in a cage to make things interesting. When I got to my new home, I smelled something else and went to the cage to check out the situation. I looked at the big-eared rabbit in the cage with a water bottle attached and wondered if that's how I'd live, too.

Needless to say, my excitement about this new situation faded for a bit.

I then saw my new bed, checked out some new toys, and got excited again. Maybe this wasn't going to be so bad after all.

My first night was a good one. I managed to negotiate my way into my SP's bed, and let me tell you – it's very comfortable. Even though she said it was just this once, I'm committed to changing her mind.

Chapter 4: Obedience Training

I was my SP's first dog, so she thought it would be a good idea for us to do some puppy training. I didn't think I needed to be taught how to be a good dog, but it meant I got to meet new dogs, so I was cool with it.

The best part about obedience training was that it involved treats. I learned pretty quickly that if I did what the instructor or my SP said during the classes, I would get rewarded with treats, so I always did as I was told.

Luckily, some of the other dogs in class were slow to catch on to what was happening. If the instructor told another dog to sit, and they wouldn't, I would jump in and do it to get their treat.

The instructor started giving me treats whenever I did as I was told, but then she realized I was following her and taking treats meant for my slower classmates.

I enjoyed messing with the other dogs in class. There was a chocolate lab in class that I wanted to be friends with, but he was too focused on what the instructor was saying, so I touched his tail, and he got startled and made a bunch of noise. At least I got him to notice me.

At the end of puppy training, my SP got my report card on how I did in the class. The teacher said I was a good student and gave me the class clown title. I'm not sure my SP was as happy as I was to be acknowledged for my efforts to bring some humour to the class, and I'm glad the instructor noticed.

Chapter 5: My Love of Winter and Dislike of Dog Clothes

Although I was born in the fall, I first experienced the outdoors in winter, which explains my love of snow.

I have so much fun hunting for goodies that are covered by snow. You'd be amazed at the stuff I find, especially when we walk through a school park.

You never know what kind of good snacks end up on the ground. I'm not picky, so I don't mind a little dirt on the treats I find.

While I love the snow, I don't like it when there's what they call a "wind chill."

Wind chill makes the air very cold, which I dislike. It's like the wind is slapping you in the face!

Whenever there's a wind chill, and the temperatures are below minus 20 degrees Celsius, I take my quickest walks, focusing on my bathroom needs only!

The more snow, however, the better. I like sticking my nose in it and making paw prints wherever I go, and when the snowplows make hills, I like to climb them and pretend I'm speaking to my adoring fans!

I guess my SP was trying to be thoughtful when she bought me a winter jacket. I wasn't there when she bought it to tell her it was a waste of money, so she brought it home.

I patiently entertained her putting it on me, and I was glad she was pleased that it fit. I was trying to figure out how to avoid the embarrassment of wearing a winter jacket when I saw my friends during our walks. I was mortified at the thought!

Whenever it was really cold, she would bring out the

jacket, saying it would help keep me warm. Sure, it might keep me warm, but can it hide my face so nobody recognizes me? I would start off excited to go on our walk, but once she put the jacket on me, my excitement died down—every time.

My SP would ask if I would feel better going outside without the jacket, and I would get excited because she really DID understand me!

Thankfully, whenever she tried to put the jacket on me for a walk, I would let her know I'd rather not wear it, so no one ever saw me in the coat. Even after all the trauma with the jacket, she tried to get me to wear winter boots!

I guess she didn't like being my toe de-icer when snow got caught between my toes, but there was no way I was wearing boots!

She and the boyfriend tried to get me to wear them, and I spent the entire time figuring out how to kick them off my paws. It's a good thing they kept the receipt so they could take them back.

Chapter 6: My Adventures in Leash-Free Parks

My SP introduced me to leash-free parks. We learned about them in obedience training, and my SP thought it would be a great way for me to exercise and socialize with other dogs.

I loved going to the leash-free park! Once we were in the enclosure, and my SP let me go off the leash; it was terrific. Sometimes, other dogs would chase me, and other times, I would chase them!

Honestly, I don't like playing with the smaller dogs. They talk a lot. If they start barking too much, I lose interest and look for another dog to play with. Besides, I'm used to playing with dogs bigger than me, and I don't want to play too rough and hurt one of the little guys.

One of the leash-free park's bonuses is that most people there have dog treats. I could smell them as soon as I got into the enclosure. I take a break from playtime to socialize with the people my nose tells me have the good stuff.

My approach is pretty simple: I walk up to them, sit down, tilt my head to the side, and give them a goofy grin. They comment on my cuteness, go into their pocket or treat bag, and offer me something. It works every time.

My SP likes to sabotage my treat gathering. If she spots me in action, she'll tell the treat giver that I'm shameless about treats and know how to use my charms to get them.

While that might be true, I don't see why she's ruining my fun and exposing people to my strategy. If she doesn't like me searching for the best dog treats, she should up her treat game when we hit the leash-free park, right?

Chapter 7: My SP's Boyfriend

My SP and the floppy-eared thing called a rabbit were my two roommates when it started. A few weeks after I moved in, my SP and I were on the floor, and I was getting tummy rubs when her phone rang. It was someone with a strange accent, and they were asking my tummy rubber what she was doing.

She giggled and said she had a surprise for him when he came home. He asked her if she got a dog, and she laughed and asked how he knew. He replied that he knew it was coming and then started asking more questions about me.

A few weeks later, I took a drive with my SP. It was my first airport pickup, and I was excited! However, he didn't seem happy to see me when he got in the car, which disappointed me because I thought I was meeting a new friend.

It was a rough start for the three of us. My bed privileges were revoked, and the boyfriend didn't seem to find my treasure hunts humorous. I tried my hardest to win him over, and eventually, I did!

I used my empathetic skills to comfort him whenever he came home from work feeling stressed. One of my specialties is making people feel better.

My SP never wanted to share her food with me, no matter how many sad puppy dog eyes I gave her. Still, the boyfriend always saved me some of whatever he was eating.

I learned that I had to be a good girl if I wanted him to reward me. He introduced me to fast-food hamburgers and then upgraded me to a cheeseburger. I didn't mind adding cheese and loved the burgers he would bring me.

It was thanks to him that my love for fast-food burgers started. I remember the three of us going for a car ride, and we went through a fast-food drive thru. I heard them order their food, but I didn't hear my order.

As we pulled away from the ordering station, I started to whine, so when we went to pay, the boyfriend said, "we forgot to order the dog's burger." I was so happy!

My SP's boyfriend and her mom were the best for sharing human food. I didn't have to work as hard to get food from the mom, but I enjoyed doing tricks for food with the boyfriend, even if the trick was going to my room and waiting for him to call me to get the food.

I felt special because the boyfriend never seemed to give the rabbit much time when visiting, but I could get his attention. Sometimes, he'd tell me to leave him alone because he didn't want to play, but he always fell for my sad face and puppy dog eyes.

Sometimes, when my SP was at work, the boyfriend would take me for a car ride somewhere. We would pick up my SP from work, visit with friends, and even go to his music studio.

I loved it at the studio because sometimes there'd be a man or a few, and they were all dog lovers who would give some rather good tummy rubs. Everyone at the studio knew my name, and if they were there and I showed up with my SP, they would all be happy to see me.

One night, the boyfriend left for the studio and left me at home with my SP. I was super excited when she told me we were going to the studio to bring him something he had left behind.

Once we arrived and the boyfriend opened the door, I said hello to my friends and got rubs. After a few minutes, my SP said it was time to go.

I was torn because we had just gotten there, and the guys showed me lots of love. Whenever I didn't respond to my SP calling me, she would pretend she would leave me and say, "Bye, Lulu."

As much as I didn't think she'd really leave me, I couldn't take the risk, so when she said it that night, I left my studio friends, ran to my SP and headed back home.

I loved hanging out with the guys at the studio, but my SP needed me, so I was going home to look after her.

Chapter 8: I'm a Dog of Many Names and Talents

As you know, my name is Lulu, but I have a variety of nicknames to which I respond. It started with Stinky. It then evolved into Stinky-Binks. The boyfriend calls me Ribbidy doop daps, and I'll even respond to Lulu Palulu or Lulu bear.

Don't ask me where these names came from or why I respond to all of them, but I think they enjoy it, and if I'm being honest, I do, too.

The boyfriend has a special whistle for me. Sometimes, he'd do it before entering the underground parking lot, and I'd run onto the balcony to say hi.

If there's one thing I know as a dog, it's not about what they call you but how they say it. I can tell if I'm being called for something good or if I'm in trouble.

I don't get called the nicknames when I'm in trouble. I'm just Lulu.

The boyfriend spoke a language I had never heard before, and my SP also spoke different languages.

I'm a pretty smart dog, so if either of them was giving me a command in a language I didn't know, I could tell what they wanted by how they said it.

My SP loved seeing if I could understand it when she spoke French or Spanish. I'd get many treats when I pretended I understood what she was saying. I was happy if she was happy, and the dog biscuits didn't hurt either.

Chapter 9: The Other Roommate

Living with my SP was fun! The floppy-eared thing I learned is a rabbit, which is a different story. I don't understand why she doesn't want to play with me. Whenever my SP takes her out of her room, she runs under the sofa before I can catch her!

When I catch her and put my paw on her back to stop her, she starts making whiny noises. She gets put back in her room, and my fun is over. I do get back at her, though. I take her water bottle and hide it under the sofa. When we're home alone, I grab her room and spin her around the middle of the floor.

When I had surgery done so I couldn't have puppies, the vet put a cone around my neck, and I was not too fond of it. I couldn't lick myself, especially that itchy part where I got stitches. I got frustrated one afternoon, and it was just me and the rabbit. I knocked down a plant, and dirt and pieces of the pot went everywhere.

I knew I would get in trouble, but I wasn't going down alone. I put a piece of the fallen plant in the rabbit's cage. When my SP comes home, she'll see that the bunny had something to do with it!

Another beef I had with the rabbit was that she got all the carrot shavings. I had to chase my SP on her way to the rabbit's room to grab some pieces because she'd give her ALL OF IT!

Personally, I think I got the better end of the deal. The rabbit might have gotten most of the carrots, but I got walks, treats, and sometimes, if I was really good, I got some human food.

The rabbit never got human food. Trust me. I watched closely, and the only "treat" the rabbit got with its food was something that looked like dried grass, and the food was green pellets.

No matter how much fun I tried to have with the rabbit, she never wanted to be my friend. Her loss.

The rabbit lived with us for a few years and then died. My SP seemed sad about it, and I tried to comfort her even though I didn't see it as a significant loss.

The rabbit never wanted to play with me or share her carrot peelings. At least now I can nap in the day without being interrupted by the rabbit drinking out of her water bottle.

Do you have any idea how annoying it is to hear her water bottle constantly tapping when she is trying to get water? That's why I used to take her water bottle and hide it under the couch so I could get a solid nap.

It's funny that I remember her fondly now that she's gone. She was the only one to witness my shenanigans when we had the place to ourselves, and she never told on me!

Whenever I get the carrot shavings that once went to her, I eat some in her memory—RIP, Brown Sugar.

Chapter 10: My Purpose

Do you remember when I explained what a support person was at the start of my story? I knew she needed my love and support, but when we first met, I didn't understand why.

It turns out that just over a year before I came into her life, my SP had lost her father. She had no brothers or sisters, and things with her mom had hit a rough patch.

Apparently, she was diagnosed with depression. I heard it was a coworker that encouraged her to get a dog. I also heard she'd wanted a dog since she was a little girl, and now nothing was stopping her from finding me.

When I first came into her life, she cried a lot. I like salty tears, so whenever she would cry, I would lick the tears from her face incessantly until she started to laugh. Mission complete.

Nine months after I moved in with my SP, I felt her getting sadder than usual. She was talking about her dad, and I learned that the anniversary of his passing was coming.

I knew she would be sad, and I wanted to comfort her. The night of the anniversary of his passing, I decided to be by her side while she slept, even though my bed privileges had been revoked, and I'd been replaced by the boyfriend.

I waited until they were both asleep and snuck into bed right beside her. I had to be careful I didn't fall because I was at the end of the bed, but I managed to last the entire night.

When they woke up the following day, and I was still in bed, I didn't get into trouble. They knew I broke the rules for a reason, and they both appreciated my effort to comfort her that night.

My SP is an introvert, unlike me. I consider myself a

true lover of all living things! I love meeting new people. Before I came around, she didn't know the neighbours on her floor or in the neighbourhood, but I quickly changed that.

We started with three walks a day, and I'm a social dog that likes to meet and greet everyone I pass on the street. When we got to two walks a day, we got to know the local dogs, and my SP met almost all the dog owners in the condo. Another mission is complete.

That first year was the only year I felt like I needed to sleep with her to comfort her. She had started reading a lot, which I didn't particularly appreciate because it meant less time for tummy rubs. She even started doing yoga and meditating, which I'd join in when I felt like it.

There was sadness on every anniversary, but it was never as bad as my first year with her. I'm glad I was able to help her with her grief by helping her get out of her house and meet fellow dog lovers and licking her salty tears whenever she cried.

I also felt pretty good about myself since she already had a rabbit, and she couldn't help her the way I did.

If you asked her, she would tell you I'm her favourite pet; she would never admit it in front of old floppy ears.

My other purpose was to convert people who didn't know they liked dogs. I met a few of my SP's friends who claimed not to be "dog people." I don't understand what that means, but it sounds like they don't want to be my friend.

I may not know rabbits, but I know humans. All I had to do was tilt my head to the side and give them a look with my puppy eyes, and I'd win them over.

If that didn't work, I'd give them a kiss, and they'd complain and laugh at the same time. Once that happened, I knew I'd won them over.

Just call me a human whisperer and therapist. I didn't go to any school; I got my talents naturally.

Chapter 11: My Run-in with Pills

When I first moved in with my SP, we started to go on morning jogs. A few weeks into our fun, she fell and did something to her ankle. I tried to help when it happened, but I wasn't very good at it. We slowly walked the rest of the way home.

She called to see if someone would take her to a walk-in clinic because she couldn't walk on it or drive. A friend came by, and they went to the clinic.

My SP returned with a small bottle of treats she'd give herself a few times daily. I couldn't understand why I was missing out on the special treats she got at the clinic.

A few days later, while my SP was in the shower, I decided to do something terrible. I jumped on the kitchen counter, grabbed the little bottle, and comfortably sat on the couch. I managed to get the cover off, and round little orange things fell out.

Before I managed to grab any of them, my SP came out of the shower, freaking out that I took her "pills." I couldn't let her know that I didn't eat any, and she got on the phone with poison control because it was a long weekend and my vet wasn't working.

The people at poison control told her to make me vomit. I'd done the vomit thing before, and it wasn't fun. When I first started doing car rides, I used to get sick in the car. I don't do that anymore. Car rides are too much fun!

Anyway, let's go back to my story about vomit. Poison control tells my SP to get some milk and hydrogen peroxide, mix it, and give it to me. Even though I knew what was going to happen, I couldn't help myself, and I drank some.

It didn't take too long before I felt breakfast coming up, and it did. The person on the phone from poison control was asking if my SP saw any pills. I thought that was a funny question because I only saw the food I ate earlier.

Since my SP said she didn't see any pills, they told her to take me to the nearest emergency vet clinic for a check-up. We got in the car and did the drive to the emergency vet.

The clinic told my SP she'd have to leave me there for at least a night while they worked on getting the medication out of my system. This is one of the times I wished I could talk to them to tell them I didn't have any treats and none of this was necessary.

I couldn't tell them and spent the night at the vet clinic.

My SP says it's good that she listened to her boss's stories about his wife's dog costing him a boat in vet bills and getting the pet insurance. I'm happy my medical bills didn't affect the budget for my treats!

My SP wasn't impressed when one of her friends called her, saying that she heard how living with my SP made me start a pill habit.

After all of that, I'm glad it ended with laughter, even though I still don't know what those treats were like.

Chapter 12: My Incident with a Loveseat

When I was younger, my SP used to come home from work to take me out for walks, but I didn't have the bladder control of a big dog yet. I liked our lunchtime walks because they meant that she wasn't away for too long.

One day, she didn't come home for lunch. She might have mentioned it to me, but I forget stuff sometimes. I was getting anxious about my walk and needed to release my energy.

I got tired of waiting and jumped on the leather loveseat. I slept for a bit but woke up restless and decided to scratch on the cushion I was lying on. I like the feel of leather, so I even tried to put a piece of the cushion in my mouth.

Once I succeeded, I got so excited I made a hole. I left it alone for a bit, but my SP still wasn't home, and I needed to go for a walk and get my exercise!

I got antsy, hopped back on the loveseat, and started scratching like crazy. Before long, the stuffing from the couch began coming out, and I tossed it everywhere. It felt so good and very freeing.

It reminded me of snow, and I love snow.

The stuffing looked like snow, but it wasn't the same. It didn't make my paws cold and made me sneeze when I stuck my nose in it. Either way, it kept things interesting while waiting for my SP to return. I found out later the stuffing looked like snow to my SP, too; she just wasn't as excited about it as I was.

The rabbit looked at me as if I was going to be in trouble when my SP came home, so I put some cushion stuffing in her cage so it wouldn't look like I made a mess on my own. I wouldn't take all the blame even if she was in the cage the entire time.

When my SP finally came home, I could tell from her face that she wasn't happy. She looked at me and said she had to go clear her head and she'd be back. What?!? I'd been waiting for her for HOURS; she had just returned and was leaving. I didn't even get my walk!

She wasn't gone too long. I heard later that she went to sit by the water and calm her nerves. She was apparently furious with me but realized that I was just a pup and she should have had someone take me for my lunchtime walk. So, we both forgave each other for our mistakes and moved on.

My SP used black electrical tape to try to fix the rip I had made in the loveseat, but every time someone sat on the sofa, the tape came undone.

I still liked sitting on the couch. My SP and her boyfriend (who was less forgiving and took more work to get back on his good side) started calling the loveseat Lulu's couch. Eventually, they got rid of my couch and bought new ones that weren't leather.

It didn't matter whether it was leather or not; I had grown out of my fascination with leather and had stopped chewing phone cases and shoes, so there was nothing to worry about.

The leather loveseat incident helped my SP realize that I can't be left alone for too long without some good exercise beforehand to tire me out, so I sleep most of the time I'm alone since the rabbit won't ever play with me.

Chapter 13: Visits to my SP's Mom's House

One of my favourite road trips was to my SP's mom's house. The first time we went there, the mom said she didn't have any dog food or treats to give me, which made me a little sad at first.

She then said she had leftovers and asked my SP if I'd eat the leftovers she had in the fridge. My SP laughed and said I'd consider it the best treat ever.

My SP's mom is awesome! She put my food in the microwave because she didn't want me to eat it cold. Little does she know, I'm not very picky.

I've had so much good food at "mom's" house. After the first time she fed me, I'd make a beeline for the kitchen as soon as she opened the door when we got there. I would sit nicely and wait to see what she has for me that day.

My SP seemed surprised by how lovely her mom was to me. She told me that when she was little, she was never allowed to have a dog because her parents didn't like the idea of a dog being in the house.

That seems confusing to me, too. My SP's mom is kind and lets me run up and down the stairs to see if anything changed since our last visit.

One time, during one of my inspections, the urge to pee came before I could notify my SP, and I peed on Mom's carpet. My SP wasn't happy and started to clean up immediately.

I think she thought her mom would be mad at the both of us, but she wasn't. She laughed and said she could kill me, but she didn't and fed me some more of her cooking before we left, so I think we're good.

Mom has a nice backyard that I sometimes patrol when we visit. I would announce my presence in the neighbourhood with a few barks at the local squirrels.

Sometimes, when we visit, there are sweet treats and food. Mom always gave me a piece of what my SP was getting so I didn't feel left out.

One of my favourite desserts that mom made for us was a rum cake she made at Christmas time. I had heard about this cake from my SP, and she was excited to pick one up from Mom, and I was even more excited to try some!

There's so much to tell you about my experience with Mom's rum cake that it deserves its own chapter, so stay tuned!

Chapter 14: My Rum Cake Experience

Rum cake. If you haven't had it before, you're missing out! My SP's mom would bake some at Christmas time. She always saved my SP a cake, so it was on one of our visits that I had my first bite.

It was life-changing. I'm not a big drinker, but I did drain the bits of leftover Baileys and Kahlua once and didn't mind the taste. My SP's boyfriend offered me some beer once, but I was not fond of it.

Back to the rum cake, I've heard it's got all kinds of alcohol in there. There's the stuff the fruit in the cake is soaked in, the rum added to the mixture, and the port wine poured over it every few days once baked.

I really liked the first bit of the cake I got. My SP told me not to enjoy it too much because she wasn't planning on sharing. That cake was delicious! I'd have to convince her to share some more with me or get her mom to bake me one of my own!

Once we brought the cake home, my SP tried to keep her word and not share anything with me. Thankfully, I've mastered the sad puppy look, which convinced her to give me a small piece. Not that I wasn't grateful for the sample, but I wanted more!

My SP left the rabbit and me alone at home, and I decided to see if I could find the cake. I discovered it, but my SP had stuck it in the corner of the kitchen counter, making it harder for me to get my paws on it.

I knew she wouldn't like it when I got on the kitchen counter, but I was willing to take the risk for that cake. I climbed on the counter, making sure not to knock anything off (if I was going to get into trouble, I needed it to be minor, not significant).

I managed to get the cake. It was in a plastic bag

wrapped in shiny metal. I dragged it onto the floor, and the rabbit looked away and stared at the wall while I tried to figure out how to get to the good stuff.

I finally managed to get to the cake, and I started eating it. I wasn't planning to eat the entire thing, but it tasted so good! After I ate more than half of it, my tummy started to feel weird. It felt like when I was little and in the car... yup, up comes the rum cake.

It wasn't as lovely coming up as it was going down, so I drank some water and went to bed.

My SP came home and wasn't very happy with me. She cleaned up the mess and made me go for a walk, which I really didn't feel like doing.

She complained after I did my business that all she could smell was alcohol. It's her fault; she took me out there; what was I supposed to do?

I was so happy when the walk was over. I drank some more water and went back to bed. That's all I felt like doing for the rest of the day.

My SP said I was drunk. When she tells the story, she says all I did for the weekend was drink water and sleep, just like when a human has a hangover.

After my rough time with the rum cake, my SP thought I wouldn't want to eat rum cake anymore, but she was wrong. That cake is too good!

We both learned our lesson, though. My SP found a better spot to keep future rum cakes, and I learned to enjoy what was given to me and not go looking for trouble.

Chapter 15: My Seasonal Side-hustle

My SP decided we should do morning jogs before she went to work so I wouldn't have too much energy when I was left unattended. I loved to run, especially when I was off my leash, but since I didn't have a good reputation for coming when I was called, I had to settle for jogs on my leash.

I became my SP's personal trainer while we were on our runs. I took the lead on the runs and would look back at my SP to let her know I needed her to pick up the pace when I felt she wasn't performing to her fullest potential.

I would give her breaks during the run when I needed to take my bathroom breaks and sometimes when I smelled something interesting in the grass. I tried not to let the squirrels or other dogs distract me from my work, but I didn't always succeed.

My SP agreed to run with me for as long as there wasn't any ice or snow on the ground. Every year, when we started to run, I prayed that the snow would hold off as long as possible because I enjoyed running. One year, we ran until just before New Year's Eve!

I decided I didn't want to run anymore in the spring after I turned 10. I didn't want to rush my morning outside time. I wanted to take my time and enjoy the sights and sounds.

Chapter 16: My Iron Stomach

I can eat almost anything. My SP swears I have an iron stomach because I've eaten all kinds of things that dogs aren't supposed to ingest.

The rum cake in my last story contained alcohol, raisins, and other dried fruit. My SP says she read somewhere that dogs aren't supposed to eat raisins, but I ate three-quarters of a rum cake's worth!

I've also taken chocolate that was on the table unattended. No one told me that dogs aren't supposed to eat chocolate, and everyone seems to really enjoy eating it, so I wanted to try it for myself.

I've gone to picnics and emotionally blackmailed my way to testing everything that was being cooked. My SP regretted it that night when I woke up puking, but I would do it all again if I could.

If I'm honest, I would eat anything that I could get my paws on and deal with the consequences later. Thankfully, my SP is a light sleeper and would hear when I was getting sick and take care of me.

My SP was always angry when I ate something that she was looking forward to for herself. I remember when she brought a fresh loaf of hard dough bread. She put it on top of the fridge, thinking that I wouldn't be able to reach it.

She left to get something. While she was gone, I worked on figuring out how to get to the yummy-smelling bread.

I got onto the kitchen counter, walked to the fridge, and pawed the bread bag towards me. I dragged the bread with me to the floor and ate the best part of the bread, the middle.

Sandra Dawes

When my SP came home, she was angry that I had eaten the bread and sad that she didn't get to enjoy it. I would say I felt bad about eating the bread, but it was so good that I would do it again if I had the opportunity.

Chapter 17: Getting Crate Trained

After the rum cake, the pills, and my fight with the couch, my SP decided to leave me in a crate when she wasn't home. I enjoyed my freedom and didn't like that I couldn't run around the apartment whenever I wanted to.

I blame my vet for getting crate trained. During one of my appointments, my SP mentioned she was struggling with my adventures while she was at work. The vet encouraged her to start crating me and not to look at it as punishing me but as keeping me safe. Whatever!

When she first started putting me in the crate, I thought it was a test to see if I could figure my way out. Let me tell you, I'm a pretty good escape artist. My SP and her boyfriend started calling me Houdini, who apparently was good at getting out of impossible situations.

The first couple of times, I impressed myself with how fast I could break out of the crate. When my SP came home, she was never as happy as I was about my accomplishment. I guess I wasn't supposed to go on investigative adventures around the house.

My SP realized that I needed a sophisticated system to keep me locked in my room. The pinch clips that came with the crate were no match for me. I just had to jiggle the door with my paws, and the pins would pop out. Easy-peasy!

It's not like my room was uncomfortable. My SP even gave me toys and a comfy cushion to make it enjoyable. I didn't like the idea of being confined alone with a rabbit locked up in her cage.

The thing is, there's only so much sleeping a dog can do! Especially when I can't hide the rabbit's water bottle, and she can keep me up with her constant drinking. I will never understand why she needed to drink from a bottle with a metal ball, not from a bowl like me!

Eventually, I grew to like my crate. It was where I'd go when I didn't want to socialize with anyone. I could go to my crate, hang out with my stuffed animals, chew toys, and nap whenever I felt like it.

The bonus of being left in the crate while my SP was at work was the treats I would get before she left. My SP hooked me up with a frozen Kong packed with peanut butter and my dry food. I LOVE peanut butter, which could last me a couple hours. If she wanted to give me more than one of those daily, I'd be a happy dog!

As much as I missed the freedom of being crate-free, I didn't miss the trouble I'd get into when the adventures I went on in the day while my SP was at work made a mess. I don't believe it's my fault the rabbit never wanted to play with me, and I didn't know how to turn on the television. I was just trying to entertain myself until my SP came back home.

Chapter 18: My Boyfriend

My SP got me "fixed" before I was six months old, but that didn't mean I lost my interest in boys. I liked playing with male dogs that were bigger than me.

Once I became an adult, I weighed about 45 pounds. On one of my walks, I met a dog more than twice my size—a black Giant Schnauzer—and I was in love!

My SP and his people would see each other in the park, and he was so well-behaved that sometimes they walked him off-leash in the park. When his people saw my person, they asked if she wanted to let me off the leash to play with him.

I'll admit that I didn't always return to my SP right away when we were alone, but she always trusted me for a playdate with my boyfriend. I loved being chased. I'm a fast runner, and some people have called me "Pocket-Rocket" because of my size and speed.

My boyfriend would chase me, and once he caught me, we would wrestle for a bit. When we first started playing like this, my SP would always be worried he'd accidentally hurt me when he jumped on me.

Still, he was a gentle giant, and I loved playing with him. As soon as he jumped off me, I'd jump up and want to play more.

I once saw him on his way to the park when my SP and I were headed past him. Before he saw me, he was carrying a tennis ball in his mouth, and when my love saw me, he spit out the ball and waited for me to greet him.

We met and played for several years, and then he disappeared. We finally saw his people, and my SP asked where he was. They said he got sick and was diagnosed with cancer and had to be put down.

I was heartbroken! I was never going to play with him again. Eventually, his people got another Giant

Schnauzer. I played with him, too, but it wasn't the same. He looked like my boyfriend, but he didn't smell like him and didn't play with me the same way.

He was my favourite playmate. I've played with big dogs at the leash-free park, but it was never the same as it was with my true love.

Chapter 19: My Naughtiest Moment

Okay, so I've already shared some of the antics I was up to while growing up with my SP, but now I have to confess what I think is the worst. If you speak with my SP, she might have a different experience in mind, but it's my story, so I'm telling you my version.

When I was young, say, 2 or 3 years old, my SP sometimes let me off the leash at the park. I loved the freedom to explore without a leash. It meant I could chase squirrels without worrying about hurting my SP and find food!

One morning, we went out for our walk. When we got to the park, my SP took the leash off my collar so I could run and tire myself out before she went to work (yes, this was after the leather loveseat debacle).

To my surprise and excitement, I found a turkey bone in the park that morning. I'm not talking about a leg or a wing; I'm talking about that big centrepiece. Unfortunately, no meat was left on it, but it tasted nice.

When my SP spotted me with the bone, she ran towards me, telling me to drop it. I didn't want to drop it. It tasted nice, and I knew if I dropped it, she would pick it up and throw it away. If you're wondering how I knew, I learned from experience.

For some reason, my SP was against me eating street food. Whenever I found something tasty, a chicken leg, a donut, a cookie, or a piece of bread, as soon as I put it in my mouth, I would hear my SP say, "Drop it."

Most of the time, I didn't want to drop what I had in my mouth, so she'd grab my snout, open my mouth, take the goodness out, and throw it far away so I couldn't find it. I had made up my mind that she wasn't going to ruin my fun this time.

Every time I made myself comfortable with my turkey bone, my SP would come and try to take it away from me. She was getting frustrated because she had to go to work and still needed to go home, shower, and change clothes to get ready for work.

She got so fed up with me that she told me she was going home to prepare for work and would come back to see if I was ready to go home. I didn't take her seriously. She'd never left me alone on my own outside before.

That's how I learned to take "Bye Lulu" seriously. She actually left me in the park with my turkey bone! She said she'd be back, so I continued to enjoy my bone while she was gone.

She eventually returned, dressed and ready for work, but I wasn't done enjoying my bone yet. My SP decided to call her friend, who had stayed with me for a day while she was at an out-of-town meeting a few months before.

I really liked her friend. She gave me lots of treats while we were hanging out watching television. My SP knew this and thought her friend could get me to come to her.

Once I heard her friend say my name, calling me to come to her, I got so excited I dropped the bone and ran to see her. My SP stood beside her and put the leash on my collar while I got rubs from her friend.

It was a long time before I got leash-free privileges again. I'm glad I got to enjoy the turkey bone for longer than my SP wanted me to, but I'm also happy she came back for me (as if there was any doubt!).

Chapter 20: My Bad Habit

If you ask The Boyfriend, he'd probably say my worst habit is my constant need for food. If you ask my SP, she'd say it was my pulling.

I can't help it. When I get outside and I see something interesting, I start to go towards it. Unfortunately, I'm on a leash, so I end up pulling my SP. I couldn't pull if The Boyfriend was walking me; he was too strong.

Sometimes, it was a dog on the other side of the road. Other times, it was another animal, like a squirrel or a cat.

One day, I was out for a jog with my SP. We always ended our jogs with a sprint home. As we were running home, I saw a dog across the street and wanted to say hi.

It was early morning, and the roads were pretty busy, so when my SP saw the dog across the road, she held tight to the leash. Still, I'd been running pretty fast, so she slid on her knees on the grass to stop me from running into traffic (and taking her with me).

I heard her telling someone the story, saying she felt like she was sliding into home as she slid on the grass to stop me. I've never watched baseball, so I don't know what that means, but I'm glad she found it humorous.

My bad habit has led my SP to try numerous leashes on me. I've worn a harness, another one that was supposed to mimic my mother scolding me, and others that had to be replaced because of another bad habit I have, chewing things I'm not supposed to.

I know I shouldn't pull, but sometimes, I just can't help myself. Whether it's another dog, a squirrel, a rabbit, or anything that moves quickly, I want to go after it. It's not my fault I love to socialize!

Chapter 21: My Relationship with Water

I'm not a fan of water. I'd prefer not to go for a walk if it's raining outside, but my SP makes me.

I don't like baths either, so I'd be very dramatic if my SP tried to give me a bath. I would grab onto her shirt like my life depended on it.

She gave up and started taking me to a groomer. The professionals knew how to get me to relax; they gave me treats to make the water bearable.

My SP and the boyfriend used to take me to a nearby lake. They always tried to get me in the water, but I wasn't interested.

I kept hearing that I was supposed to be a water dog. My SP said something about my webbed toes and quick-dry coat, but that didn't mean anything to me.

My curiosity made me willingly enter the water for the first time when I was six. I saw a beautiful white bird sitting on the water and wanted to get a closer look. I knew the only way to do that was to get my feet wet.

Once I started to go in the water, my SP and the boyfriend got excited to see me and began cheering me on. I thrive on doing things that make them happy, and I realized that being in the water wasn't as bad as I thought it would be.

After I came out of the water, the boyfriend picked up a stick, and I got excited to play fetch. He threw the stick in the water, and I ran in and got it. I was getting as wet as I would if I went outside for a walk in the rain, but I didn't mind.

What started as a fear of the water became a love for it. Don't get me wrong, I still don't like walks in the rain, but whenever I'm in the car and smell a lake, I get excited and want to play in it.

It's weird how something that seemed scary for so long can actually be fun! Who knew? I never got to meet the swan that got me in the water, but I'd sure like to thank him or her if I got the chance.

Chapter 22: I'm a Lover, but I Do Have Nemeses

As a social butterfly, I get along with most people and dogs. Some dogs have chosen not to be friendly with me, even when I've tried, for whatever reason.

My first nemesis is a Doberman Pincher. Whenever she saw me, she'd get aggressive and start pulling on her leash, showing me teeth. Maybe she was jealous of my calm nature. The poor man who had to walk her tied her to a metal fence to pick up after her because she was so unpredictable.

When she first started aggressively barking at me, I would take it personally and start barking back. My SP told me I was picking a fight I'd more than likely lose because she's a bigger dog. I agreed with her and let it go since I didn't want to stress out my SP with unnecessary vet bills.

I meet my second nemesis in the next chapter of my adventures, but I'll include him here because he belongs on my list. I move into a new neighbourhood with a big backyard and many new dogs to meet. This dog and I lived on the same street, and it seemed we had the same walking schedule because we'd always bump into each other.

When I first saw him, both his owner and he didn't seem very friendly. The dog growled, and the owner pulled him away. There was no "hello" or a chance to sniff his backside!

It rubbed me the wrong way, as they weren't interested in being friends, so I would tell him off every opportunity I got. Whether I was on a walk or saw him while I was spending time in the backyard, they would both get a good tongue-lashing for not being friendly.

I don't understand it; being nice doesn't cost anything.

Chapter 23: My Own Backyard!

I lived in a condominium for the first 11 years of my life. You can imagine my excitement when my SP took me for a car ride, took me to a yard, and told me it would be my backyard.

I sniffed and checked it out and thought it was pretty cool. There was only one fence at the back, and I could run around the house's perimeter if I wanted to. The boyfriend ruined those dreams when he had one of his friends build a side fence and a gate to keep me in the back.

I still loved the backyard. It was pretty big, and I got to chase squirrels, rabbits, and all kinds of birds. I even watched dogs that would pass by my yard and let them know that a new dog was in the area.

My SP and I met new people and dogs. I befriended a woman who always had treats while walking her dog. Whenever I saw her, I made a point of saying hi, so she gave me a treat. Her dog didn't seem to mind; I guess he liked to share.

By then, I had started getting grey hair on my chin, and my SP called me Greybeard. When people saw us on one of our walks, they sometimes asked my SP how old her puppy was.

She would laugh, say I was no puppy, and tell them my age. Everyone seemed surprised when she said my age because I still acted and felt young. I was energetic until the end.

After I enjoyed my first year in the house, I started not feeling well. Sometimes, walking or running hurts my hips. I had difficulty maintaining my balance in the winter when it was slippery outside.

My SP cared for me; even though we had a backyard, she would still take me for walks. She'd let me do my business in the backyard if it was freezing, so I didn't have far to go to get back inside.

I really liked my new house. I loved having more room inside and a big yard to play in outside. It was the best way to spend my senior years.

As much as I enjoyed my new home and yard, I knew I wouldn't be around to appreciate it for very long. As energetic as I was, I was starting to feel tired, and it was taking a lot more effort to keep my balance on the winter walks; I was even falling in the house.

One day, I slipped and fell in the house and couldn't get up. I knew it was a sign that the end was coming, and I didn't want to trouble my SP and the boyfriend, so I just laid down and stared at the wall.

I heard my SP asking for me, and when she saw me, she asked what was wrong and went to get me a treat. That was her way of testing how I was because if I was good, I wouldn't say no to a treat, no matter what it was.

When she came to give me the treat, I didn't want it and turned my head away. I heard her say, "Uh-oh," and the boyfriend asked what was wrong. My SP told him I wasn't taking the treat, so he tried, but I still didn't want it.

They tried to take me for a walk, but I couldn't tell them I couldn't get up. My SP tried to stand me up, but I fell again. The boyfriend took me outside to pee, and he had to hold me up to do it. I just couldn't stand up by myself anymore.

When we returned inside, my SP told the boyfriend we had to go to the veterinary hospital in the morning because she didn't think I would last long. They both seemed sad and slept with me in the living room that night.

Sandra Dawes

The following day, nothing changed, so we drove to the clinic and waited for the vet to see me. When it was my turn, the vet checked me out and told my SP and the boyfriend that my heart rate was weak and slowing down.

He asked them what they wanted to do, and my SP said she didn't want me to suffer anymore and asked the vet to put me to sleep. The vet agreed it was the right choice and went to get what he needed.

My SP and the boyfriend started crying and telling me how much they loved me. Usually, the boyfriend didn't want me to kiss him, but I decided I had nothing to lose and gave him a goodbye lick on his cheek. He didn't seem to mind that time.

I hoped my SP was going to deal with me leaving healthily. We had done all that work to get her out of her depression, and I'd hate that to happen again, but I was confident that the boyfriend and the work she'd done while I'd known her would give her the strength she needed.

I didn't want to leave my people, but I knew it was time, so I didn't fight the feeling and let the forever sleep take over. I hear they cremated me and put some of my ashes in the lake where I took my first swim and have the rest in a box. I wonder what they'll do with the box.

Chapter 24: Wait, There's More!

Did you think my story was going to end with my death? Of course not!

Six months after I left, my SP and the boyfriend decided to get married! It only took them 18 years, but I was happy to know it was happening.

I dreamed of being the Dog of Honour at my SP's wedding, or at least the ring bearer, but it wasn't meant to be. Six months later, they got married on a beach in Jamaica.

They'd abandoned me a few times to go to Jamaica, and I missed my opportunity to experience it for the wedding (they would include me if I was still around, right?).

I also heard that they've now moved to Jamaica! I think my not being around anymore gave them the freedom to make a big move like that. I wonder if they would have brought me to Jamaica with them.

It doesn't matter now because I'm not there anymore. I do miss my SP and the boyfriend, and I know they miss me because I hear them talking to or about me almost every day!

I didn't think I had such an effect on them. I know I still think about them daily, and sometimes I even try to send them signs that I'm thinking about them.

They haven't gotten another dog yet. I hear them talking about it occasionally, but they haven't done it. I don't think I'll be jealous if they get another dog; I'll just be happy for the dog because I know it will receive lots of love.

I'm grateful for my time with them, and I believe I fulfilled my purpose for my SP. She was much stronger when I left her than when I found her, and that's all that matters.

Chapter 25: I Made it to Jamaica!

A year after my support person and the boyfriend (now husband) moved to Jamaica, they came back to Canada and decided to carry more of their things back with them, including my ashes!

While I thought it was nice of them to want to have me around for their new chapter, it wasn't very long before I started to wonder if this was such a good idea.

I was listening to my support person watching something on her phone when she mentioned a storm named Beryl.

I didn't know storms could have names, but from the sounds of it, big storms deserve their own names.

There was a lot of discussion about how to prepare and what was needed from the storms. I've been through thunderstorms and snowstorms, but this seemed more serious.

The winds started to get strong, and I heard the front door fly open.

The boyfriend, now husband, ran to close it and told my support person to disable all the electronics and secure my ashes in a safe place.

The husband put some spiritual music on his phone for protection, and that was playing for most of the storm while his phone battery lasted.

Obviously, my ashes are in the box, but my spirit can still see what's happening. The storm was pretty scary. The door flew open a few more times in the next 90 minutes, and a lot of water came in.

My support person gathered every towel they owned to stop the water from coming in from the bottom of the door, even when it was closed. Once she did that, she mopped all the water that had come in.

When I saw the husband holding the door, it reminded me of a show I used to watch with my support person, Game of Thrones. He was holding the door against Beryl like Hodor was holding the door. I won't say anything else if you haven't seen it yet—I don't want to spoil it for you!

I have to admit that the time after Beryl seemed quite grim. There was no electricity, the phone signal didn't always work, and many people lost their roofs. I wish I was around to share some kisses and try to lift people's spirits, but there was nothing I could do.

I'm glad I wasn't there physically to experience the hurricane, even though my support person was making jokes and laughing to lighten the mood while she was mopping the floor and the husband was holding the door. I'm glad we made it through it all safely!

I think that now that things have settled down and power's back, I can make myself at home properly.

From what I've overheard in conversations, I think a new dog will soon be in their lives. I can't wait to see him or her and see if they are anything like I was.

Who knows? I may keep you posted with stories about their antics! ☺

Author Biography

Sandra Dawes is a freelance writer including ghostwriting. She holds an Honours BA, an MBA, a certificate in Dispute Resolution, and is a certified Master Life Coach.

She enjoys spending time with friends and family and her husband Satnam. She published her first book Embrace Your Destiny: 12 Steps to Living the Life You Deserve in 2013, which is based on her journey with depression after the death of her father.

Sandra was added to the Wall of Role Models by the Diversity Advancement Network in July 2016.

She continues to write for her blog, www.sandradawes.com.